≪PETER AND THE WOLF≫

SERGEI PROKOFIEV

Translated by Maria Carlson

≪ PETER AND THE WOLF ≫

ILLUSTRATED BY CHARLES MIKOLAYCAK

The Viking Press
New York

To MATTHEW, *who likes pictures, and* to LINDA, *who likes music.* ⟪C. M.⟫

Early one morning Peter opened the gate and walked out into the big green meadow. In a tall tree sat Peter's friend, a little bird. "Everything is calm and quiet," the bird chirped merrily.

Waddling behind Peter came a duck. The duck
was delighted that Peter had not closed the gate, and
she decided to go for a swim in the deep pond in the
meadow. Seeing the duck, the little bird flew down,
sat on the grass beside the pond, and shrugged.
"What kind of bird are *you* if you can't fly?" she

said. "And what kind of bird are *you* if you can't swim?" the duck answered. And she plopped into the pond. They argued for a long time, the duck swimming around the pond, the little bird hopping along the bank.

Peter suddenly noticed a cat stealing through the grass. The cat thought, That bird is busy arguing, and now is my chance to catch it. Silently, on velvet paws, the cat crept toward the bird.

"Look out!" Peter called out just in time, and the little bird quickly fluttered up into the tree. The duck quacked at the cat angrily from the middle of the pond.

The cat paced around the tree. Is it worth climbing up that high? he thought. By the time I get up there, the little bird will have flown away.

Peter's grandfather came out of the house. He was
angry because Peter had gone past the gate into the
meadow. There were dangerous places out there. What
if a wolf should come out of the woods?

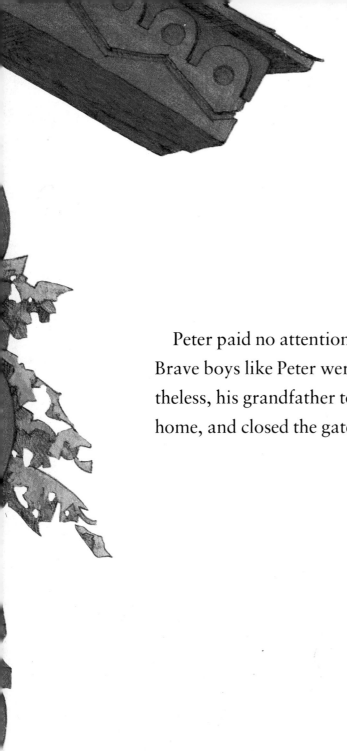

Peter paid no attention to what his grandfather said. Brave boys like Peter were not afraid of wolves. Nevertheless, his grandfather took Peter's hand, led him back home, and closed the gate firmly.

Just then a huge gray wolf did come out of the woods. The cat quickly climbed the tree. The duck quacked and scrambled out of the pond. But no matter how fast the duck tried to run, the wolf ran faster. He came closer... and closer...he caught up with her...he grabbed her... and swallowed her.

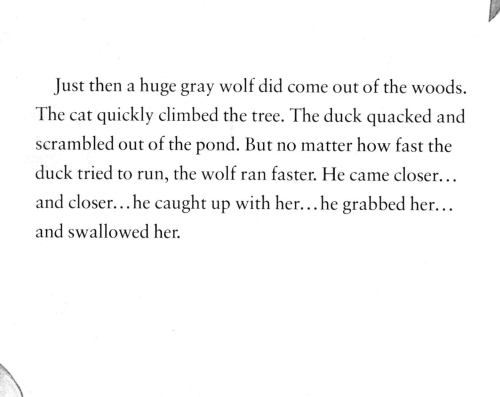

Now the cat perched on one branch of the tree, the little bird on another, farther away from the cat. The wolf paced around the tree and looked up at them with hungry eyes.

Peter, who stood behind the closed gate, had seen everything that had happened, but he wasn't at all frightened. He ran home, found a heavy rope, and then climbed up on the high stone wall.

One of the branches of the tree reached as far as the wall. Peter grabbed the branch and nimbly climbed into the tree. He said to the little bird, "Circle around the wolf's nose, but be careful not to let him catch you!"

The little bird flew down and almost touched the wolf's nose with her wings, and the angry wolf jumped every which way. Oh, how the little bird teased the wolf! How the wolf wanted to catch her! But the little bird was quick, and the wolf could do nothing.

Peter made a loop at the end of the rope, lowered it slowly, caught the wolf's tail in it, and pulled tight. The wolf knew he was caught, and in his rage he jumped about, trying to free himself. But Peter tied the other end of the rope to the tree. The more the wolf jumped, the tighter he pulled the rope around his own tail.

Just at that moment some hunters came out of
the woods. They had been tracking the wolf and
were firing their rifles. Peter called to them from the
tree, "Don't shoot! The little bird and I have
already caught the wolf! Help us take him away to
the zoo."

And so they did. Just imagine the triumphant procession: Peter walked in front. Behind him came the hunters, leading the wolf. Peter's grandfather and the cat came last. Grandfather shook his head with displeasure. "And what if Peter had not caught the wolf?" he said. "What then?" Above them flew the little bird, chirping, "Hurrah for Peter and me! Just see what we have caught!"

And if you listen very carefully, you will hear the duck quacking in the wolf's stomach. For the wolf in his haste had swallowed the duck live.

Thanks to Ann, Carol, Davida, Dominik, Friso, George, Harvey, Jack, Jim, John
Judy, Lance, Liz, Margot, Maria, Martin, Radio Budapest, Susan, Tomasz, Torgny,
Traudl, Wolf, and to Alec G., Alec M., Angela, Arnold, Arthur, Basil, Bea, Bob, Boris,
Brandon, Carlos, Carol, Cyril, David, Eduardo, Eino, Eli, Elma, Frank L., Frank M.,
Garry, George, Gerard, Henk, Hermione, Hudson Actors, Jacqueline, Jacques B.,
Jacques M., Jean, Jerome, Jimmy, Johnny, Jose, Karlheinz, Lasse, Leon, Leonard,
Mathias, Mia, Michael, Natalia, Paul, Per, Peter, Preben, Ralph, Richard B., Richard
H., Rob, Sean, Sterling, Sven, Tom, Trond, Viv, Will & William.

First Edition
Illustrations Copyright © 1982 by Charles Mikolaycak
Translation Copyright © 1982 by Viking Penguin Inc.
All rights reserved · First published in 1982 by The Viking Press, 625 Madison
Avenue, New York, New York 10022 · Published simultaneously in Canada by
Penguin Books Canada Limited · Printed in U.S.A.

1   2   3   4   5   86   85   84   83   82

Library of Congress Cataloging in Publication Data
Prokofiev, Sergey, 1891-1953.   Peter and the wolf.
Translation of: Petia i volk (narration)   Summary: Retells the orchestral fairy tale
of the boy who, ignoring his grandfather's warnings, proceeds to capture a wolf.
[1. Fairy tales]   I. Carlson, Maria. - II. Mikolaycak, Charles, ill.   III.
Title. PZ8.P947Pe   1982   [E]   81-70402   ISBN 0-670-54919-3   AACR2